ANACHRONY

TIMELESSNESS
BOOK 3.5

Susana Imaginário

ISBN: 978-1-7398202-0-6 (paperback)
ISBN: 978-1-9161402-9-5 (ebook)

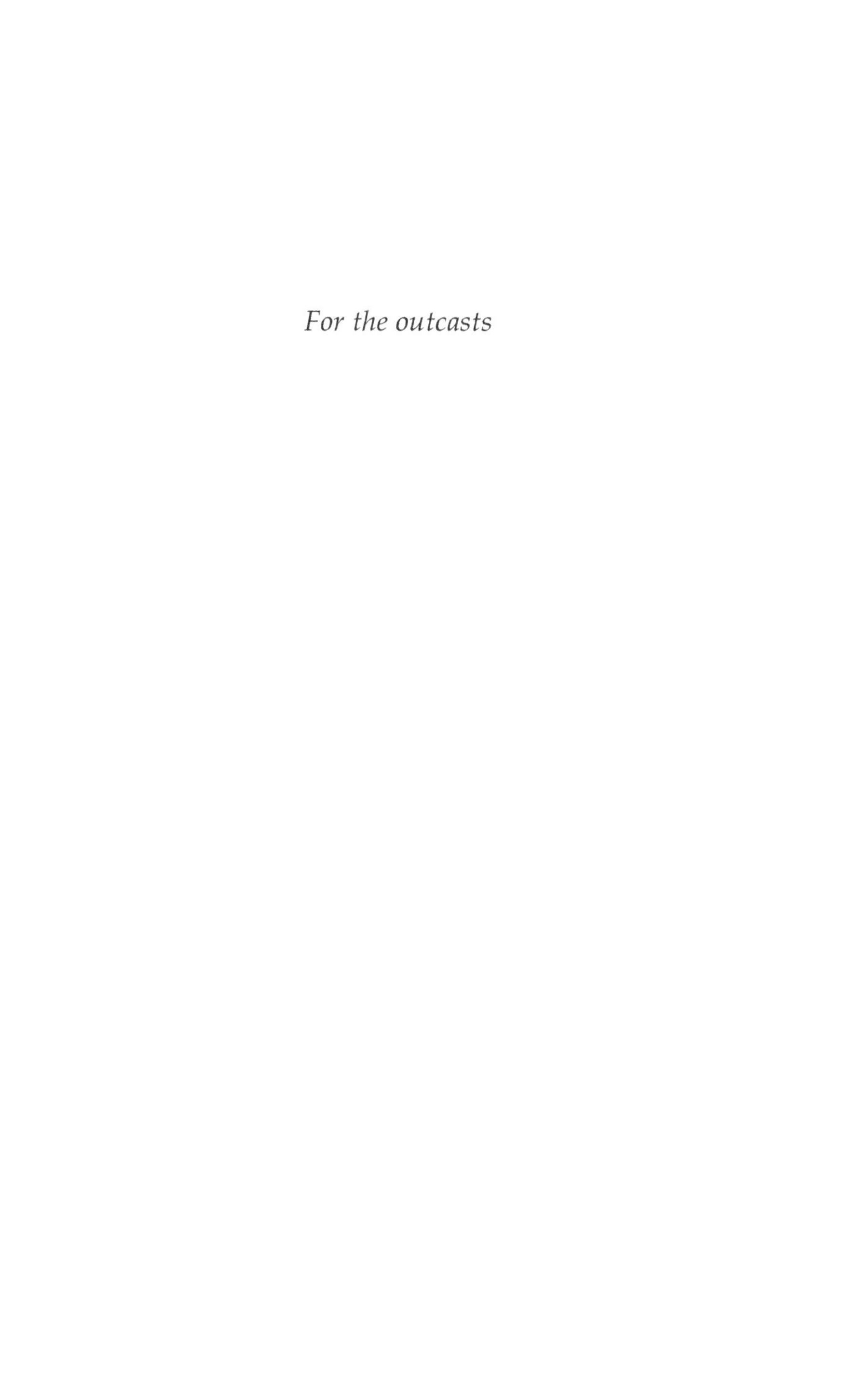

For the outcasts

Note from the Author

When I first wrote Timelessness, a mid-series novella was not part of the plan.

The events described in Anachrony were originally written as interludes of Nephilim's Hex (Timelessness Book 3), but as I was revising the book, I realised they kept breaking away from the narrative and shifting the focus from the main plot points in the story. I then tried to include these events in Anamnesis (Timelessness Book 4), but the same problem occurred, so I rewrote and expanded the story until it became a sort of interlude for the series. (Timelessness 3.5)

Anachrony still relies heavily on the events from the previous books, and it shouldn't be read on its own. However, I hope it will answer a few questions for those who read this far and keep the story alive in their minds until Anamnesis comes out next year.

Thank you for reading!

Susana Imaginário

I

Arianh wakes up screaming, but she makes no sound.

She can't speak, can hardly breathe in the searing heat. Something feels stuck in her throat; she tries to cough it out and fails. Her mouth is dry; her shrivelled tongue seems to belong to someone else. She moves it over her cracked lips, and their skin rips apart with the abrasion. She tries to speak again.

"Waaa – Aaah! Ow..." She changes her mind and focuses on opening her eyes instead. The sun is bright – too bright and extremely hot on her bare skin. Yet she feels cold... Her bones are freezing, her skin burns and the muscles, caught between the two extremes in temperature, cramp painfully.

What's happening to me?

'*What you wished for,*' says a genderless, ageless voice inside her head.

Arianh coughs again, moans in pain and would have cried, too, had she any tears to shed. Her eyes are so dry, she winces rather than blinks every time her eyelids scrape over them.

Blood oozes from her gums; the metallic taste makes her gag. She tentatively runs her tongue across her teeth and finds two of them broken. They hurt. So do her cheeks and her hands, her head, even her skull. Everything hurts!

Calm down, she tells herself between deep breaths, spitting out bloody saliva and trying to figure out how this happened.

There's dirt on her gums mixed with the blood. And something else, something resinous, it tastes like… *Oh goddess!* She remembers. She remembers the Titan Chiron digging in the earth beneath Yewlow with her, both racing to find the Ambrosia buried there. She remembers his face when she finds it first, and she can almost feel his hands still on her cheeks, prying her jaws open mercilessly after she, in a thoughtless moment, put the resin in her mouth. She remembers Agnar shouting, cursing, begging for them to stop fighting, then begging for her to let him have it.

I swallowed it.

Arianh cringes. It all went dark after that.

She tries to move. Her muscles respond in spasms. She's hot and cold, numb and excruciatingly sensitive all at once. *And why the frost is it so freezingly bright?*

She lifts her hand to shield her sore eyes from the blinding light and squints at her surroundings. There's no Titan, no Agnar, no forest, only a gnarled tree and dozens of forlorn boulders scattered about the parched landscape. She's never seen so much nothingness. Not even the Gharb is this desolate, and that's saying something.

Of the torrent of questions running through her mind, one becomes prominent: *Where am I?*

'You are exactly where you were before; when you wanted to be,' the voice replies dispassionately.

Oh, goddesses, no!

A black bird flies overhead, casting a brief shadow over her before landing on a crooked branch next to another bird, identical to itself.

"Huginn, Muninn?" Arianh croaks.

"Caw!" the ravens reply in unison.

The tree – if it can be called that – is withered and leafless. Its spiralling black bark peels away in chunks like dead skin under Arianh's touch. Most of its trunk is hollow, and yet she's able to sense sap still flowing glacially slow through it as if it's her own lifeblood.

"Yewlow…?" she asks disbelievingly.

'Yes?'

Arianh's stomach constricts. She bends over to retch its contents on the tree's exposed roots. The mixture, mostly composed of bile and a partly digested peach she'd picked on the way to the Chronodéndron, is instantly absorbed by the cracked soil, leaving only a piece of chewed pulp to dry out under the blazing sun.

"What happened?" she asks, but of course she knows what happened. *How* it has happened is what Arianh really wants to know.

'What usually happens when someone lets their heart rule over their mind,' the tree replies matter-of-factly.

Arianh wipes her mouth on the back of her hand and grimaces. Her fingertips are raw and covered in dirt. Most of her nails are broken, one is gone, another hangs by a thread of skin from her index finger. Arianh gapes at her trembling hand as, ever so slowly, a thin layer of tender skin begins to cover her fingertips and new nails grow to replace the ones lost until she has a recognisable hand again. She closes her mouth, licks her lips and tastes no blood. The soreness in her cheeks is fading, and her teeth are no longer broken. She laughs.

It worked. Ambrosia worked!

'*Of course it did. Everything worked as you wished,*' Yewlow says.

Still mesmerised by her hand, Arianh replies, "Yes," and then, "No! I did not wish to come to this place, or time, or whatever *this* is. Take me back. This is not what I wished for!"

'*I'm afraid I cannot,*" Yewlow replies patiently. "*Here* is *what you wished for. Here is where you belong.*'

"The frost it is!" Arianh shouts to the tree. "I did not wish to travel here, or anywhere, for that matter. I demand you take me back now." She thumps her fists against Yewlow's trunk as if the tree is a bolted door and she has to get it open. It's a stupid thing to do, of course. In her experience, that never actually works on doors, let alone trees.

Think, Arianh! You can fix this.

She places both hands on the tree, takes a deep breath and forces herself to visualise Yewlow as she'd last seen it: young, lush and ugly, with Chiron lying in its shade, wounded and desperate. Agnar, frail and afraid, standing by her side. In her mind's eye, Arianh sees how the fading daylight creates long shadows around them. She can almost smell the stink of the Titan's corrupted wound mixed with the fresh evening scent of the forest, taste the bitter soil in her mouth. She even recalls how the worm wriggled against her cheek and down her throat as she swallowed it. And she wishes it all to be real, to be happening again.

Take me back to that moment. I pray, wish, beg of you! she pleads to the tree.

Something akin to sympathy touches her mind.

'I am sorry, Arianh. One prayer needs to be fulfilled before another can be made.'

"Nooooooo!" she howls: a loud, harrowing cry of frustration and regret.

The ravens fly away.

II

'*Arianh!*' Yewlow shouts.

Arianh jerks to alertness. She's holding her head in her hands and immediately her fingers, tangled in her hair, curl into claws, gripping at the roots, and her nails dig into her scalp. Having someone screaming directly into your mind takes some getting used to, even under the best circumstances. In these it's a test of her sanity.

No wonder the gods are all crazy and cranky if this is their usual way of communication, she thinks bitterly, untangling her fingers from her hair to rub her sore eyes.

'*You must move into the shade,*' the tree says.

Arianh squints numbly at her surroundings. The golden sun overhead emits unbearable light and heat, painting the world yellow and making the air shimmer as far as the eye can see. Her bare skin has turned an unflattering shade of pink, like a Dharkan's under Apollo's sun. She holds her breath. *Who the frost is Apollo and how do I know the blue sun is his?* she asks herself. But she already knows the answer. She knows it because Yewlow does. And a whole lot of nothing that information is worth to her now.

She blinks. *Shade, yes, I should find some shade.*

She'd fallen into a stupor after her breakdown, but now she mostly feels stupid for having to be told what to do like a child. She hisses and curses as she crawls her way over the scalding dirt towards the rocks nearby. One of them lies tilted across another, providing enough shade for her to hide beneath, sheltered from the noxious light.

Once there, she starts praying. She prays to Hel first, for this is still her world, after all. When she gets no answer, she prays to Hades. Still no answer. She prays to Odin next, then Gaea, Psyche, Chiron, she even prays to Chronos! None of them answers.

"Where is everyone?" Arianh asks the Chronodéndron. The sadness reaches her just before the answer.

'You should try to get some rest. Tomorrow we'll talk.'

The overwhelming sense of helplessness almost makes her cry again, but she's too tired and dehydrated for tears, and so she falls asleep instead.

∞

She wakes up with a sneeze, teeth rattling with cold.

"Freezing goddess!" she curses, wrapping her arms around her torso. The temperature has changed drastically. Now instead of struggling to breathe in the heat, Arianh shivers, breath puffing in the cold air.

Where am I now? For a gleeful moment she thinks she's back inside the Stump during one of Aedan's icy moods, but her senses quickly disabuse her of that hope. She's still beneath the rock she dragged herself under earlier, with Yewlow not far away, judging her from inside her own mind.

"How long have I slept?"

'Not long.'

Just long enough for the blazing sun to run its course across the sky and take the heat of the land with it, apparently. Only a few rays remain shining from behind the Shadow Mountains like dying embers in a neglected hearth. No ice or snow covers their black, angry edges. They look smaller without snow. More like ill-shaped boulders piled together to form a craggy wall rather than a mountain range.

'Get up,' Yewlow commands. *'It's time to go.'*

"Go where?" she asks, rubbing her arms for warmth.

There are stars in the sky above her, but Arianh had never really paid much attention to the stars, so she can't tell if they are the same ones from her time, let alone guide herself by their position. Still, there seem to be an awful lot less of them than she remembers.

'You'll need to hydrate soon, or you'll die.'

Arianh almost laughs. She'd die from cold long before she died from thirst in this weather. "I can't die," she says bitterly. "I ate Ambrosia."

'Ambrosia spares you from decay, not death,' the tree chides. *'Now, get up.'*

She doesn't. "And who the frost are you to give me orders?" her royal pride demands.

'I'm your tree. My life is now linked to yours. As you wished.'

"I did not wish for this!" Arianh protests. Of all the things running through her mind before she travelled, linking with Yewlow was not one of them. She is sure.

Something akin to amusement runs through their link. *'You don't even know your own mind, Arianh. You wished to be more like your mother. She was linked.'*

"She was…?" This is news to Arianh, as were most things she learnt about her mother since she passed away.

'Now, for the last time, get up and walk towards the sunset.'

The command is uttered in such a way, that this time Arianh obeys almost reflexively. Maybe walking is not such a bad idea. It should keep her warm, at least.

"What's at the sunset?" she asks.

'Water.'

III

Arianh walks all night. She walks until her feet are numb, her legs cramped, her lungs burning. She walks until she no longer feels the cold, the exhaustion or the pain, and every time she thinks she can't walk any further, her body surprises her with one more step, one more stab of agony endured, one more gasp for air. That's the real power of Ambrosia, she realises: to prolong life and therefore suffering. Her mind consumes itself with questions and regrets as she walks, but Yewlow refuses to communicate with her beyond the occasional command to change direction or pick up the pace.

By dawn, all her thoughts have converged into one: death. Not just physical death, but a complete cessation of being. She wants to stop. Stop walking, stop breathing, stop feeling, stop thinking. Just stop. Nothing else matters to her anymore. Not the Suzerain, not her people, not immortality, not her sister, Agnar or Judoc. It all becomes too small and meaningless with each agonising step. The only thing that matters to Arianh now is the pain and the need for it to stop.

Please make it stop, she prays again and again to anyone who might be listening.

There is never an answer.

'*Over there*,' Yewlow finally says, just as the first rays of daylight pierce the grey sky. '*Follow the dried riverbank. There's still water pooled under those stones nestled against the base of the cliff.*'

Arianh very much doubts it. The sand under her feet is as dry as dust, but she does as she's ordered, for make no mistake, Yewlow is not *asking* her to look under the rocks; the tree's will is a compulsion as inexorable as Arianh's situation.

Upon closer inspection, it's clear the stones covering most of the basin nestled against the cliff have been neatly piled together by something other than nature. Arianh manages to move a few of them aside with some difficulty (Ambrosia does nothing to improve physical strength, sadly) and finds, as she expected, more dry sand underneath them.

'*Keep digging*,' Yewlow says.

And so Arianh does, for at least while she's digging she doesn't have to walk. And maybe if she digs deep enough, she can use the hole as her own grave. The foolish morbidity of her thoughts makes her lips twist into a rueful smirk. *Goddess, I'm losing it. I'm as batty and hopeless as a Wyrd.*

After long moments scrabbling in the dry sand, moisture touches her fingertips. *Could it be?* She digs faster.

"Water! I found water!" It's murky water, but still – *water!* Arianh presses her lips to the sand and tries to suck the moisture directly from it. The result is a mouth full of mud and a reproachful *tsk* from Yewlow.

Arianh spits out a few interjections of her own and keeps digging until something like a puddle forms inside the hole. It takes her until close to sunrise to hydrate fully, but once she has, all her pains – mental and psychical alike – are gone.

Thank you, she says to Yewlow, lying back on the sandy bank, breathing deeply.

'We're not out of the woods yet – metaphorically speaking. There is quite a long way to go.'

Of course there is… Arianh thinks but doesn't move. She just lies there, enjoying the few moments of rest and pleasant temperature before the oppressing heat returns. It doesn't last long.

The sun appears overhead, revealing the extent of the utter desolation around her. Arianh is still in Aegea, all right. She recognises the outline of the landscape well. The once lush and overpopulated land is now empty and dry. There are no trees, no settlements, no rivers, no lake, no mists and barely any clouds – exactly as Judoc had described it to her. She hadn't believed him back then. Not really. The man was always prone to exaggeration, especially when he was trying to get a woman's attention. But not about this, it seems. To her surprise, thinking of Judoc brings none of the usual emotions. No anger, no grief, not even lust. Only a brief pang of guilt at having so easily dismissed his accounts and a fleeting wonder about how much of his personality resulted from having grown up in such an environment. Perhaps all of it, but it hardly mattered now.

The lack of emotion is refreshing and welcome. She didn't realise until just then how tired she's been of feeling for the man. Besides, she now has more pressing feelings to overcome, such as the sunlight licking her skin like flames.

I must find shade, she tells herself, realising she knows exactly where it can be found. A hundred or so paces uphill, there's a small hollow in the cliff wall. She has no need for Yewlow to guide her there. Their minds are linked, after all. The problem is interpreting the link. Yewlow's mind works very differently from her own.

'You need to suspend your own thoughts and perceptions of the Universe in order to perceive mine and learn all the things I can teach you,' Yewlow explains once Arianh is safe and sheltered.

Ah, is that all I need to do? Arianh thinks sarcastically, curling herself inside the rock. *Well, in that case, wake me up when the lesson is finished.*

IV

Arianh wakes up blind. At least that's what she thinks because it's pitch black, but not cold. Her other senses tell her she's not alone.

"Good, you're awake." The woman's voice is hoarse and aged and very much *not* inside her head.

Arianh sits up with a start, startled and utterly confused. A dim light appears in front of her eyes, illuminating the room.

The room?! Her awareness protests. It is indeed a room – of sorts – with stone walls, no windows and a few steps leading to a hatch in the ceiling. The kind of room Narrum like to use to store their food – and their prisoners.

"Where am I? How did I get here?" Arianh asks, pressing herself flat against the wall, away from the light and the wrinkled, outstretched hand holding it.

'I guided you here while you slept,' Yewlow says.

Can you do that? A stupid question. *You had no right to do that!*

'You said not to wake you.'

That was not what I meant!

There's no point in arguing with her other self right now. How Arianh got here is secondary to the fact that she *is* here.

"Who are you?" she demands.

The old woman remains silent while she leans closer to study her face like a cat studies an injured bird.

Arianh gasps in surprised horror. The woman's skin is deeply burned and leathery, but there's no mistaking her race. *Dharkan.*

"Freezing goddess!"

The woman cackles to herself, shaking her head. "I never imagined an insult could feel so much like a compliment."

Arianh isn't amused. She never imagined Dharkan could age! And whoever this creature is, she's definitely not Hel. "Who the frost are you?" she demands again.

'*Someone you can trust.*' Yewlow's words are reassuring; the way the Dharkan crone stares at her, however, is not.

"I asked you a question," Arianh insists petulantly.

The woman's smile is disdainful, with an edge of pity. "Once a queen, always a queen, hmm? I should know," she says with a wink.

Traces of a beauty long lost are still visible beneath the old woman's damaged skin, and her frail body still shows the sort of prideful bearing so common in royalty. She wears a thick open-ended gold necklace around her scrawny neck and a cloak made of shiny black feathers over her bony shoulders. It makes Arianh think of Odin's ravens. *Where would they go in this harsh land? How could they survive?* She looks at the cloak again. *Oh goddess!* Maybe they didn't. She tries to slide along the wall, further away from her captor, but there is nowhere to hide inside the room. The only exit lies behind the ancient Wraith and, weak as she might seem, Arianh knows she has little chance of getting past the creature.

"That attitude won't do you any favours in this time, so I suggest you drop it," the woman says in a tone that ices the blood in Arianh's veins.

She opens her mouth to argue; the old woman lifts a finger, and the words die in her throat.

"I am Freya. But you can call me auntie, if you prefer."

Arianh blinks. "Why would I?"

"You used to call my husband uncle," the old woman says with a twinkle in her pale blue eyes. Arianh isn't sure if she's amused or offended by this, since her emotions are all mingled with Yewlow's. More disturbingly, she had no idea her uncle was married. He never mentioned a wife, and she never thought to ask. Arianh never thought about so many things, she now realises. Her mind has always been occupied with the wrong thoughts.

"Are you a Wyrd like he was?" Arianh knows gods hosted by Dharkan are not Wyrds; they keep their powers, and the light shining between them proves it. She asks the question anyway to buy some time to make sense of the creature.

The old woman inhales deeply before replying, "Not quite," then she sets the light hovering above their heads with a flick of her fingers and begins rummaging furiously through a tattered sack at her side.

"Are you alone?" Arianh asks. Freya should not have been able to use her talents without her host's consent. This means the female Dharkan is either compliant, dead, or too far gone to object.

"No, dear. Far from it. There are others, many others still lingering about."

This was not the answer Arianh had in mind, and her eyes dart around the gloomy room as if expecting to see them. "Where?"

Freya shrugs. "Oh, most have been hidden away for so long they've become part of the landscape; others are in abeyance and hopefully will remain so until the Universe freezes. You don't need to concern yourself with them, only with the ones still stuck in the Underworld. And, of course, the living."

"There are people *living* in this dust bowl?"

The goddess exhales. "Yes, isn't that what I just said?" She seems genuinely confused.

Arianh wonders again how much time has passed. It was one of the many questions she asked Yewlow the previous day while she walked, but the tree pretended not to understand the question. '*Time is not a cloud,*" she replied mockingly. '*It doesn't pass. Time is the sky above the passing clouds.*'

Arianh tries a different question.

"Are, er... Hel or Hades still in the Underworld, then?"

The Dharkan goddess curses, not slowing her search. "No. The Underworlds belong to a god from another pantheon. It's a fire pit now, with no character and no purpose but to inflict suffering on those condemned to it. Again, you don't need to concern yourself with that, for only those with souls end up there."

"What about –"

"Too many questions, girl!" Freya snaps, getting frustrated with the sack and whatever she's looking for inside it. "Sometimes learning too much about the past is as bad as learning too much about the future, especially in your case. Yewlow will educate you, when the time comes. Right now, we need to make you anew. You can't walk around wearing that face."

Arianh touches her cheeks, worried she might be freckled like a Narrum from the harsh sun. She hasn't seen her reflection lately, and obviously she can't be looking her best, given the circumstances. Still, there is no need for the crone to be so rude. She's far from a pretty sight herself.

"Don't be afraid, I'll make you beautiful," the old Dharkan says patiently, as if guessing her fears, then finally takes a wooden box from the bag. Inside it is a chisel and more brushes, powders and rouges than Arianh has ever used in her entire life. Freya picks up the chisel.

"Excuse me! I am beautiful enough as I am," Arianh says, shying away from the tool poised two inches away from her nose. "And not made of clay."

"A good thing, since I'm better with flesh than clay," Freya says matter-of-factly.

"Get away from me!"

Arianh pushes the old woman aside and tries to crawl past her towards the hatch but finds herself paralysed by the goddess's will.

Let her, Yewlow commands.

The frost I will! She wants to gouge my eyes out with that thing. She's insane!

"I'm not insane. Not yet, I don't think," Freya says, obviously able to read her thoughts. "Now, stay still, Queen. And don't worry, beauty is one of my best talents."

"Is it, really? So why don't you smooth those wrinkles, huh?"

The old woman takes a long deliberate breath. "It's easier for gods to do things to others than to themselves. Besides, you are confusing old age with ugliness."

"I am not – ah!" The chisel carves through Arianh's cheekbone, nose and lips in one single cut. The pain is excruciating, but it hardly compares with the horror of imagining the consequences of that cut. The blade keeps sliding over her eyelids, slicing under her eyelashes and above her eyebrows, all the way to her earlobes. Arianh finally manages to cry out and does so until she has no voice, nor air in her lungs. Conscious through the whole ordeal, she feels every gash, every change chiselled upon her face, blood running warm down her neck to pool cold on her breasts and navel, while Yewlow murmurs calming words inside her mind.

Eventually the pain stops, and once she's done, Freya produces a mirror and hands it to her.

Close to fainting, with no fight left in her, Arianh takes the mirror in her unsteady hands. Breathing hard, shaking and surprised she's still able to see, she musters all her courage to lift the reflective surface to her face.

The first thing she notices is that her azure curls are now waves of verdant green. "What a…" Her once violet eyes have turned purple. Her beautiful small nose is gone, replaced with a longer one matching her new higher cheeks and wider mouth. Her full lips are no longer able to pout properly it seems, but then again, they have no need to. She touches her face. The combination is aesthetically surreal, making her look much younger and yet more feminine somehow, the way goddesses often like to present themselves. She looks confident thanks to her new eyebrows, while the shape of her eyes simultaneously conveys shyness and assertiveness. Arianh never truly understood how much the shape of one's face can influence and even determine how others interpret their personality until this moment. Overall she remains beautiful, yes, perhaps even more so than she was before. She just isn't her. To make things worse, the reflection reminds her of Ileana and her father. She almost laughs, except nothing about it is funny.

"What have you done to me?" she mutters. Her voice remains the same, thankfully.

"I've made you anew," Freya says.

Tears form in Arianh's new eyes. "Why…?" she sobs.

"It's the price of immortality, my dear." There's a hint of reprehension in the old woman's voice. "And a necessary one for survival amongst mortals. Even gods need to change their faces from time to time if they know what's good for them. Lesson number one: You can live many lifetimes, just never as the same person."

Arianh looks at herself again, not knowing how to cope with what she sees.

"You want to go back to when you came from?" Freya asks.

"Yes! More than anything."

"You want to save your people?"

"Yes," Arianh says, less enthusiastically. The truth is, she only wishes to save herself at the moment. Whatever altruism she had was likely left in the past or cut away by the old hag along with her smile.

"Then wear this." Freya takes a heavy coat from the sack. It looks like it was stolen from a Narrum's corpse. It probably was, judging by the awful stink of it.

Arianh pushes it away with a sniff. "It's disgusting."

Freya narrows her eyes. "Less disgusting than raw skin and a fair deal warmer than rock. It's at least five full days' walk from here to the Gharb. Ambrosia will only repair so much, so I suggest you wear it."

"The Gharb? You want me to go back to the Gharb?!"

"It is what I just said. Do I need to do something about your hearing?"

Arianh covers her ears when she sees the crone pointing at them with her chisel and shakes her head.

"Just take the accursed coat and stop assaulting my mind with thoughtless questions. One would think I cut through your wits instead of your skin."

Arianh takes the coat, tries to pout and almost starts crying again.

Freya gathers her things back in the sack. "We'll keep in touch."

"How?"

"Yewlow can Reach me. Do exactly as she says and you will succeed."

"In what?"

"Making things right."

Arianh's jaw slackens. "I –"

"Here, take this." The old goddess hands her a crooked obsidian dagger. "You might need it. And if you don't. Give it to Ileana. She definitely will."

Arianh's jaw drops further, then picks itself up. "Ileana is here?"

"Not yet." Freya puts the bag over her shoulder and walks to the precarious ladder. After a short climb, she pushes the hatch open. The sound of its rusty hinges makes the pain in Arianh's head blossom into a migraine.

"I suggest you wait here until nightfall." Freya doesn't wait. She climbs the last steps of the ladder and slides through the narrow opening with a limber agility at odds with her appearance.

"Why are you *helping* me?" Arianh asks from the bottom of the ladder. She has to force herself to articulate the word *helping*, given that she feels more hindered and brutalised than ever.

The goddess sighs at the threshold and speaks without meeting her gaze. "Because it's all I can do. Like you, I too wished for the wrong things. That mistake cost me everything and everyone I ever cared about. There's no fixing my mistake, but yours may still be undone, and by doing so it might make mine less devastating."

"So… this is not part of Chronos' punishment for my offence?"

The goddess chortles, a bizarre thing to witness in a Dharkan. "No, dear, Chronos isn't offended. He's gone."

The hatch closes, leaving Arianh in darkness and silence.

V

Arianh sits at the bottom of the ladder, playing with the tips of her new hair as she tries to process it all. Travelling was a mistake, an unintended accident, and yet Freya seemed to have been expecting her. Yewlow had no problem admitting she'd taken her to the Aesir goddess, but she refused to explain why. Thanks to their link, Arianh has access to the tree's thoughts and so she knows there's a lot more the Chronodéndron isn't telling her. But trying to read her mind is like trying to read one of Seshat's books: she could see it, hold it, open it, flip the pages, trace the script with her fingers, smell it even, and yet none of those things made her any wiser about the information written there. She knows one thing, though: a god's interference in mortals' affairs, regardless of their intentions, is troublesome enough when they carry them out in the open, but when they do it in secret and in disguise, it means they are acting behind another god's back. Usually a much more powerful or resourceful god. It seems no matter what Arianh does, where or when she goes, there's no escape from their schemes. She's nothing but a pawn to them, and immortality has only made it worse.

"I'm so stupid…" she murmurs to the walls while she cries. She can't pout, but she can still cry at least. Yewlow doesn't like when her thoughts spiral into self-pity. Well, tough. Maybe trees are beyond such weaknesses, but she still feels the need to express her pain. Someone has to grieve her loss, damn it. Even if it's herself. And where the frost has Yewlow taken her, anyway?

Something catches her attention beyond the mental fog caused by her misery.

"I hear footsteps," she whispers.

'Ignore them,' Yewlow says.

The tree then strongly suggests she stay there and sleep until she's told otherwise. But how can she sleep after what happened? Never mind the freezing, hard marble floor. Her backside is so sore and cold it's as if it belongs to someone else, like her face. No, Arianh decides, she's had enough of the Chronodéndron's *suggestions.*

"I'll just have a look," she says, her hand inches away from the handle on the hatch. A sense of resigned disappointment runs through their bond, but Yewlow doesn't protest, and if she can stop her, she doesn't. Arianh figures this means whatever is moving above can't be too dangerous or too important. She pushes the hatch.

Glaring light blinds her. The heat wave is so intense it nearly knocks her off her precarious perch. Arianh loves warmth, and being born and raised in the Gharb, she's more used to it than most dryads, but this is beyond her tolerance. It reminds her of the furnace she found inside the Stump, relentlessly ablaze. Absently, she wonders if the gods ever found out its power source or purpose, then shakes her head and closes the hatch with a loud thump. "Freezing goddess! This is not natural."

"Who's there?" a male voice demands from outside.

Arianh jumps off the ladder, misjudges the distance in the dark and twists her ankle upon landing. *Frost, frost, frost!*

'Well done.' The trees tuts.

Of all the trees in Aegea, why did she have to link with a Chronodéndron?

The hatch opens, flooding her grim cell with smouldering light. Arianh hops backwards, hand raised to shield her eyes from the glare.

"Who the frost are you? Where did you come from?" demands a male dryad wrapped in a tattered cloak. He has angry, bloodshot eyes, shining amber through thick eyelashes under furrowed brows beneath the heavy hood.

"A –"

'*Ann,*' Yewlow says.

What? Arianh asks, confused.

'*Tell him your name is Ann.*'

"Are you deaf, girl?" the man demands.

"Ann," Arianh mumbles, squinting at the light and the sight of him. She'd never seen a creature so old. Even Freya, with all her wrinkles, appeared youthful in comparison. Dryads don't age – not like Narrum do, anyway. The patterns on their skin eventually harden to leathery patches, and their hair can turn black and thin, but this man is nearly bald, his skin cracked like pine bark. He's beyond old; he's ancient.

"Huh?" he says, tilting his head, obviously the one hard of hearing.

"My name is Ann, and I came from" – she hesitates – "the Gharb."

Yewlow approves.

The man frowns, pulls a flask from inside his heavy cloak and rubs the sleeve of his robe on it thoroughly before taking a sip, without moving his gaze off her. "You're a long way from the Gharb, woman. How did you even get here?"

"I walked."

The old man takes another mouthful while contemplating her answer, clearly unconvinced. "Did Iva put you in there?" he asks.

"Who?"

He puts the flask away. "Freezing Wraith! She has no right to use my shelter as her personal pantry. Come out of there!" he says rather harshly.

"Into the sun?" she says, suddenly reluctant to abandon the shade and the false security of the stone walls.

"Are you Dharkan?"

"Of course not! Do I look like –"

"For a dryad who claims to have walked all the way from the Gharb, you are overly concerned about the sun, so you're either a Dharkan or a Wyrd. Come out so I can see which. My eyes are not what they used to be."

Arianh is about to protest again but thinks better of it. He's right. She's a dryad, and dryads shouldn't fear the sun. Besides, she has Ambrosia. If she survived being butchered by Freya, she can survive a bit of sunburn, and she can't stay inside that hole forever, anyway.

The man, frail and hunched, looks harmless enough. Still, she grips the dagger tight in her fist for reassurance before concealing it away in her foul garment, determined to defend herself if the need arises. There's no fighting the sun's light, however, and Arianh curses halfway up the ladder, skin already burning with its energy.

"Well, well. You do look and sound like a dryad," the man says, scrutinising her from under his hood. She barely listens, awestruck as she is with their surroundings.

Huge marble pillars stand all around them, some still intact, most crumbled in dramatic ways. The ruined remnants of a dome provide some shade a few yards away, and she can swear she glimpses something green growing behind an archway. The overall design of the ruined structure resembles the temple in Relicum, except this is much larger and older than any structure she's ever seen apart from the Stump.

"What is this place?" Arianh asks, looking up and about her with her mouth agape.

"This is my sanctuary. You're trespassing on it," the man replies with annoyance.

"I-I didn't mean to," she says, hopping from one foot to the other.

He scowls at her. "Are you sunstroked, woman?"

"No," she replies with indignation. "I'm just hot." The stone under her feet is scalding the soles of her feet.

She almost forgot how it felt to be warm during her time inside the Stump and certainly never thought she could ever be uncomfortable in the heat. How wrong she'd been. It would be better if Freya had given her a pair of sandals instead of a coat. No, better if she hadn't shown up at all! Goddess, but every bit of skin exposed to the light felt about to blister.

"Such a delicate flower, you are," he mocks. Easy for him to say, all wrapped up in thick cloth and leather boots.

"How can anyone even feed in this light?" she wonders aloud.

She'd once witnessed a Narrum forcing her child to eat more than she was willing to, claiming the food would otherwise spoil and they might not have a chance to eat another meal for days. The poor child cried and gagged while the mother shoved morsels of meat into her mouth under the threat of physical punishment. Eventually the child threw up and received a beating anyway. Arianh figured basking in this sunlight must feel similar to being force-fed beyond what your body can take. Except she wouldn't be able to purge the excess. It would just build inside her instead, making her sick.

"In small doses, of course," he replies. "Hey, where do you think you're going?"

"Shade," Arianh replies, limping her way behind a pillar.

He shuffles after her. "You really didn't like your mate, to run all the way here, huh?"

Arianh winces at him. "What? No."

He tuts. "Whatever the reason, you're better off there. No one survives here. It's only a matter of time before the Narrum catch you, rape you, and put you on a spit over a cookfire."

The image makes her grimace. "How come you're still alive, then?" she asks.

He opens his cloak and pats his left leg. It makes a strange metallic sound. "I'm not to their taste." He laughs.

"What's so funny?" Arianh asks, unable to take her eyes from the old man's mouth. He's not only bald but also toothless.

"I couldn't explain it to you even if I wanted to," he says. Then he steps closer, tilting his head to the side again. "You sound familiar. Like a voice in a dream or a memory. I do not recognise your face, but… there is something…" He frowns. "What did you say your name was again?" Arianh opens her mouth, and he waves a leathery hand in front of it. "You know what, never mind. You're a woman, and women are not welcome here. Go, away with you. I don't like company." He opens his arms wide and tries to shoo her away as if she's a chicken. The man has obviously spent too long in the sun.

Arianh tiptoes behind another pillar to put more distance between them. "And where is *here*, exactly?"

"This is the grand temple of Portum, of course," he says proudly, arms spread wide as if trying to embrace the entire structure.

Arianh squints. The temple is grand, all right. Or was at some point. But she sheltered in Portum's temple many times, and this isn't it. Or could it be? She studies the surrounding area. "It looks… different," she murmurs.

"From what?" he asks.

"From what I remem – from what I imagined, I mean."

"Everything does." He speaks grudgingly, casting around. "I know it's hard to imagine, seeing it now, but this was once the greatest temple ever built in Aegea. Mortals built it, believe or not, and for a short time even Wraiths sheltered here along with the living under this very roof." He scoffs. "But of course that didn't last. No matter how great the sacrifice or how strong the alliance against evil, there's always something stronger to break it, just as no matter how grand the structure, nothing can overcome the forces of nature. Time destroys all things," he says with such heartbreaking sadness she expects him to cry at any moment.

"How long has it been since…?" Arianh isn't sure how to finish the question. Since its construction, since the Wraiths? Or since the world ended?

He gave her a quizzical look, a sort of puzzlement mixed with abhorrence. "Leave." The word a cold wind cutting through the heat. "Go back to your little peninsula before time swallows you too. You'll find no shelter or salvation here."

He drinks from his flask again and turns away.

Arianh licks her lips, eyeing that flask. She's thirsty, getting thirstier the longer she stays in the sun, and the idea of walking away in the searing heat does not appeal to her one bit.

"Wait," she says. "Apologies. I did not mean to trespass on your sanctuary. I was just looking for shade."

The old man waves a firmly dismissive hand.

Yewlow, feel free to chime in with advice or intervene at any time.

'I did offer you advice. You didn't listen.'

I hate you, she thinks to the tree. All trees are stubborn. They have to be; they are trees, after all. But even the gods know better than to argue with Chronodéndrons. Arianh figures she has a better chance of arguing with the crazy old man.

"I'll leave as soon as the sun sets, I promise. Until then, can I stay here, please? I'm so thirsty…"

He stops and sighs. His shoulders slump, and he wrings his hands around each other, murmuring something to himself. After a moment's deliberation, he beckons her to follow him under the great dome's shade.

It is in ruins, like the rest of the place, half collapsed and cracked all over. The sheer size of it makes it almost impossible to believe it was once intact, or even real. Arianh presses her hand against the weathered stone. It feels real enough. "Who built this?"

"I already told you, everyone did. Dharkan and Narrum and Anann. All working together."

"How?" she whispers. That's even harder to imagine than the actual construction process itself.

"Stop pretending you care. There is what you want. Take it." The man points a crooked finger to a recess on the far wall.

Water!

She runs to it and dips her hands into the basin,

then her face. The water is warm, murky, and it tastes of sulphur, and yet it is some of the most refreshing Arianh has drunk in her entire life. She figures it must have come from deep underground, and all things considered, that has to mean the world is not completely dead.

"Here. You don't need to carry it all in your stomach," he says, seemingly amused by her greed, and offers her an empty bottle. She promptly submerges it, ignoring his stare.

"Are you sure?" she asks while it fills. "There's not a lot of water left. I don't want to –"

He waves his hand again, cutting her off. "It never runs out. Not while I live," he says, almost regretfully, then shuffles away, walking along the edge of the dome, looking outward as if patrolling.

"How so?" *He can't be a god, surely.* Her eyes widen. *Of course!* "You are a Wyrd!"

He snorts. "No. The gods can't touch me either." He touches his artificial leg again. "So they find other ways to make me suffer."

Arianh's not sure of how to pursue the subject and she's not particularly inclined to, either. She looks around. *Goddess, what happened to this place?* she wonders again.

'*Time,*' Yewlow replies.

"Well, you can tell your God I'm not impressed with his work," Arianh says petulantly.

Something like laugher crosses their bond.

'*My god? Chronos is not my god, no more than Zeus is yours.*'

"But you answer to him," Arianh says.

'*I answer for him,*' Yewlow says.

"Talking to yourself already?" The old man chuckles. "This place will do that to you."

"Er… no. It's an old habit," Arianh admits, slightly embarrassed. It's close enough to the truth. She's been talking to herself her entire life. First because her mother forbade her to talk to anyone as a child for fear of what she might say about her, and later when she became queen because she couldn't afford to share most of her troubles with anyone for fear of what they might do with what she said. Voicing her thoughts out loud always helped her think. The only difference now is that someone actually responds. She still isn't sure if that's an improvement, though.

Her thirst sated, Arianh allows herself to relax against a crumbled wall, staring in the direction she thinks the Stump ought to be. Whatever happened in Aegea since her time, something as large as the remains of the World Tree had to remain, surely.

The man also seems to relax, or at least resign himself to her presence, sitting on the remnants of a barrel, polishing the flask in his hands – a different flask, Arianh notices.

"What happened to the Stump?" she finally asks.

The question triggers something feral in the man. He springs to his feet, eyes glistening with emotion, takes a long blade from his leg and points it at her. Arianh scrambles away as he slowly but purposefully advances in her direction.

"How stupid do you think I am?"

"I –"

"You almost fooled me with your looks and your tricks. Did they put you up to this? Did Morpheus?"

"I really don't – frost!" Arianh narrowly dodges the blade as she runs past the crazed creature.

"I'm not on your side!" he shrieks. "I'm not on anyone's side. Never been and never will be. They can't have me! Do you hear me?" He chases her across the ruins with a great deal more agility than she anticipated, and it's all she can do to keep him at a safe distance.

"I do! I hear you loud and clear."

He stops, exhaustion finally catching up with him. "I'm on *my* side," he murmurs before crumbling down. "Go away. Leave me alone. Take your water and go. Do not come back. There's no one here to give you answers."

Yewlow, now it's definitely a good time to chime in.

'*Do what he says.*'

The man's shoulders shake as he sobs. He looks as helpless as a child. "No one's side…"

'*You can't help him. Not in this time,*' Yewlow says, reading Arianh's thoughts.

There has to be something I can do. He's obviously distressed. Let me try to comfort him, at least.

'*No one can comfort him, Arianh. Take a good look, for that's what happens to mortals when they turn their backs on their kind as well as the gods. They become kings of their own ruins. We have enough water to reach the Gharb, so rip the fabric off your sleeves and wrap it on your feet, put the coat over your head and start walking.*'

Arianh spares one last glance to the crazy old man. She doesn't really care much about his suffering, but she cares even less about walking all the way to the Gharb in these conditions. She'd rather stay in the shade with a pool of foul-tasting water nearby and figure out what the frost happened to the world. Yewlow won't let her stay, though, not with any peace of mind, and Arianh fears the tree will take over her body if she disobeys. And so, with a heavy heart and a long-suffering exhale, she does as she's told and simply walks away.

VI

Arianh takes in what used to be her kingdom and sighs.

Tell me again, why am I here?

'*It is the curse of time to repeat itself. And those who travel its path always need to come full circle before they can move on,*' Yewlow replies cryptically.

It's been days since her arrival at the Gharb, and unlike Arianh, the rocky peninsula hadn't changed much. It takes a long time for rock to change, and the ocean doesn't seem to change at all. That's how the people living on its shore survive. The Aossi had long learnt not to rely on rain, for it never rained in the Gharb. Arianh only figured out why after the gods took over the Stump and discovered the Suzerain's powers were linked to Zeus and that he'd used his talents to create the nightly storms over Aegea. The storms weren't just for show. Narrum dislike rain, therefore the torrential downpours kept most of the population indoors during the night, and the Dharkan dislike light, so the constant lightning impaired their vision, making it difficult to hunt. Meanwhile, the Grove grew lush for the Anann dryads – his chosen ones – while the Gharb grew arid as punishment to the Aossi for resisting his rule. Instead of relocating or praying for rain, the Aossi figured out how to use the sun to distil the salty ocean water by patiently gathering condensation, drop by drop. Water was the Aossi's currency, not metal or pretty stones, which was another way they were at a disadvantage when dealing with the rest of the population in Aegea. It was the price of freedom, yet it was no wonder so many of her people abandoned their freedom to live in fear in the forest or settlements and refused to bring children into a world where they had to work so hard for mere trickles of moisture.

Still, the parched land ahead barely resembles the memory of that harsh realm.

Arianh stares up at the horrible yellow sun and wonders who's controlling the weather now.

The most depressing and highly distressing thing about the Gharb in this time, however, is not its desolation but the people living in it. They call themselves Anann, not Aossi.

It seems her people have been completely overrun by the dryads of the Grove and settlements. None even recognises the word Aossi.

Agnar was right. How could this have happened?

'It happened because you left them,' Yewlow says.

It was a rhetorical question! Arianh snaps. No wonder the Wyrd considered killing their hosts a mercy. The last thing anyone needs in a hopeless situation is a voice inside their head constantly reminding them of their mistakes.

Yes, misguided or not, Arianh left her people, and now here she is, ready to make amends. How, exactly, she hasn't figured out yet, and no one is telling her either, despite constant assurances that she will and bids to remain patient.

Patient... Arianh scoffs. If her wish was to be more like her mother, this is not the way to fulfil it, for she's been anything but patient. Is Arianh supposed to lead these people now? If so, how and to where? Days have passed since she arrived at the Gharb, and Freya still hasn't sent word. And all Yewlow's words do is aggravate her moods. The longer she stays, the less she knows what to do with herself. Besides, these people already have a leader.

The Anann welcomed her with open arms and asked no further questions about her identity or origin after the mention of the dreaded Chronodéndron. She wasn't the first cursed by the tree, they explained in sympathetic tones. Apparently, many others travelled through it over the years. Most simply wandered off to the Shadow Mountains or were found shattered on the rocks at the bottom of the cliffs. Arianh suspected, by the way the people spoke and acted around her, that they were trying to avoid that particular mess with her.

She was so lucky to cross the ridge without encountering the Narrum hunters – the Anann told her with wide eyes and hands covering their mouths. Of course, luck had nothing to do with it. Through the eyes of the ravens, Freya kept Yewlow – who in turn kept Arianh – appraised of the Narrum's every movement and location during her journey.

Upon arrival, Arianh introduced herself again as Ann. Yewlow insisted the new name was more appropriate for the time, and Arianh's new face remained blank at the suggestion. She has no title or identity in this place. What is a name after she already lost herself?

The Anann provided Ann with her own shelter and plenty of water. Not privacy, though. They followed her every move and checked in on her constantly, making sure she was 'comfortable'. They were curious, of course they were, but this behaviour was prompted by caution, not curiosity. They only talked to her when she approached them first, and even then, the conversation rarely expanded beyond the weather, which shouldn't have been a topic at all since it never changed.

It soon became clear there was more to their behaviour than caution and fear for her sanity, though. While eavesdropping on a group of children, she found out that no one had authority to question chrono-travellers. That task fell to their leader, and so her status remained somewhere between guest and prisoner while they waited for him to return and tell them what to do with her.

The leader in question had left with a scouting party the day before she arrived. The Anann men spent many days at the time patrolling the borders and setting traps for the Narrum. The trepidation amongst the people increased with every passing day of his absence. These people were terrified of the Narrum, more than any creature should be, but they seemed to be afraid of losing or displeasing this authority figure even more. Like abused children, the Anann lacked the will to act for themselves, always afraid of doing the wrong thing, whatever that might be.

Arianh suspects they have to be under the will of a god, or a Wyrd. Hopefully, one who doesn't know her.

VII

Arianh's returning from the beach after a long swim when she sees the commotion. Everyone has left the shade of their shelters and abandoned their tasks to greet three young men – little more than boys, really – coming down the narrow path to the centre of the settlement. They're naked apart from the thick hides over their heads, the rags around their hips and the sandals on their feet. Gaunt and sunburnt, they grin and wave enthusiastically at their cheering families and friends, shouting their names in joyous greeting. One stands out from the others, striking even at a distance. An elderly man walks up to him and, after a few words, points in her direction. Their eyes meet, and the impact shatters her.

Goddess, no. Please, no. Not this.

In truth, it doesn't come as a complete surprise at this point. The knowledge was there, hidden in Yewlow's mind. Arianh just didn't care to look. She had no need to, same as she had no need to look at a corpse to know it was dead by its stink. She seriously considers turning around, walking back to the waves and swimming into the horizon until the world serpent claims her, but she remains rooted to the rocks under her feet by a will stronger than her own.

'*This is why you're here,*' Yewlow says.

I did not wish for this.

A deep sadness crosses their bond. '*You wished to be loved.*'

Not by him!

'*You wished to be loved, and you wished to be relevant to the gods' plans.*'

I thought Chronodéndrons were portals, not wishing wells.

'*We take travellers to their heart's greatest desire.*'

Horseshit. This is not my desire and you know it. This is Chronos' doing.

'*It is. But even he can only work with what he's given. To wish is easy. No one ever takes into consideration the ramifications of their wishes. Deep down, you always feared this would happen, and you've done what you could to avoid it. Time is inexorable, and so are the things you work so hard to avoid; otherwise, you wouldn't feel the need to.*'

Arianh shuts her eyes to hold back the tears. Yewlow is right, as always. In hindsight, every decision she's ever made has brought her here – to him. To this moment.

'*You know what you have to do. I suggest you do it right,*' Yewlow says.

He's handsome, Arianh has to give him that. Tall and lean. The patterns on his skin follow the lines of his muscles in sensual harmony. He has a stern face with well-defined masculine features on the verge of perfection, a long nose, and intelligent eyes. His dark green hair pulled back and tied with string has yet to turn black at the temples, and there's no malice or cynicism in his smile yet either. Still, she would recognise Alek Dveer anywhere, at any age.

For his part, it's almost love at first sight, and no wonder. Freya carved her face to match the woman of his narcissistic dreams, a female version of himself. Still, Alek isn't easily distracted, and answering his questions without raising suspicion takes more than a pretty face, coy smiles and bashful looks. She's always been able to manipulate men with those. Not him, though. Smitten or not, Alek's first conversation with her isn't a courtship but a thorough interrogation of her and her origin, and the man is anything but gullible. Fortunately, he is also no match for three minds working together with the shared knowledge of the past, present, and future.

Once Arianh earns his trust, making him fall blindly in love with her is easy, one could even say, inevitable.

And she would spend the rest of her life regretting it.

Alek is one of the few Anann who still believes in gods, and to his mind she's a gift from them. The irony of it is that, in a way, he's right, and she does her best to not disappoint him or raise his suspicion to the contrary.

Things move fast between them. Procrastination was never part of the Anann culture, after all. And for its leader, the pressure to select a woman to breed with is coming to a head. If he spends any more time away to avoid the duty, he'd better become a scout permanently and give leadership to a more family-oriented man.

To that effect, Arianh soon becomes pregnant. After she's given birth, picking the name for the baby girl is also easy.

"Ileana," Arianh says, looking at her newborn with mixed feelings.

"It's like you read my mind!" says Alek, bursting with happiness.

All her life she's wanted a man to look at her the way he does now. Just not this man. Why couldn't she have been more specific about her wishes?

Can I go now? she asks Yewlow every day since Ileana was born.

'*Not yet, I'm afraid,*' the tree always replies.

And so Arianh's spirit shrivels a little more with each passing day.

'*A wise woman once said the secret to happiness is not having what you want but wanting what you have once you have it,*' the tree suggests, sensing her misery.

Arianh tries to follow the tree's advice. After all, Alek is a good lover, a good husband and a devoted father, but try as she might, she can never love the man he is, knowing the man he will become.

Over the years, she becomes withdrawn, stretched thin between the person she is and the one she once was. She focuses on Ileana, her daughter – the idea never quite fits inside her mind – for she will be the key to saving the past and consequently the future. Sadly, every time she looks at the girl, she sees the woman she met in Judoc's arms, and the more she tries to teach her to think for herself, the more she pulls away towards her father's ideas. To him, Ileana is the brightest star in the universe, and the more Arianh withdraws, the more his obsession for the girl grows. And the girl loves him back. To her, he's a god. No wonder. Whatever Ileana demands and Arianh refuses, he gives it to her. Whenever she says no, he says yes.

I'm not cut out to be a mother, Arianh confides to Yewlow in frustration after one such occasion.

'*Few are,*' the tree replies matter-of-factly.

Arianh doubts it. What does a tree know about marriage or raising children, anyway? None of the other women in the Gharb seem to share her troubles. To them, failing at motherhood is akin to a crime against nature, and they are much more keen on punishing her than helping her, for they envy her place. Had she not been married to Alek, she would probably have been exiled already. And so a tree is the only one Arianh can trust to share her thoughts. Day after day she tries to fit into her role. The harder she tries, the harder she fails. And not just at motherhood.

Alek is not only a good father and husband but a good ruler too: fair, attentive, hardworking. No one goes thirsty or unsheltered in the Gharb. He always makes the best out of their meagre resources and has a keen instinct for tracking the Narrum. He's brave and loyal to his people. Some days she almost forgets who he is, and she tries, oh goddess, she tries to love him back. But she can't. Even with Yewlow's influence in her thoughts, constantly urging her to forget her old life, she's never able to forget her feelings. Her own identity; her sense of self. And the truth is, as impossible as it seems, she has a better chance of learning how to be a mother and a wife than to forget she had once been a queen.

And there the greatest conflict lies.

Arianh spent her life training to be queen, and now she isn't even allowed an opinion on matters of state. It's one of Alek's main rules: women are not to be burdened with such decisions. The way he sees it, they already have enough to be responsible for: gathering water, providing shade, raising children, being there for the men. Not having to deal with politics is a privilege, not a punishment in his eyes. He just cannot fathom why she would want to sit on her ankles all day talking about traps and death and shelters and the despicable feeding habits of the Narrum. He claims she's too beautiful for that sort of thing and she has a daughter to take care of.

When confronted with her constant unhappiness, his conclusion is she must be dissatisfied with having just the one child, so he decides they should have more children to cheer her up.

Arianh makes sure she's always indisposed for conception after that.

The man truly believes women's role in life is to serve men and provide them with children, she vents to Yewlow after one of their fights.

'*Most men do,*' the tree replies patiently. '*You have an opportunity to change his mind.*'

She cannot fathom how. Alek's mind is immutable. The moment she stopped smiling and sleeping with him, she lost his love along with his respect. He never forced her, but he sure resented her, and he passed his resentment to Ileana.

Over the following years, Alek spends more and more time away patrolling the Gharb while Arianh retreats deeper and deeper into her mind, talking to Yewlow, for no one else would talk to her, not even Ileana. The girl only craves her father's presence, and she blames her for his absence. Besides, she knows whatever she says to the girl, she will then tell him.

The conversations with Yewlow grow more frequent, and sometimes she forgets herself, replying to the tree out loud. The other women begin to comment on her behaviour, the way women do when they are denied the opportunity to engage in more pertinent matters. They turn on each other with gossip.

"The sun got to her head," they say in mocking tones when they think she isn't listening.

One day she overhears a hideous woman whining to the others with malice, "She thinks she's better than us."

Certainly better than you, Arianh thinks as she walks by, smiling at their sneers. Regardless, there's nothing more dangerous than jealousy disguised as pity, so in order to avoid further hostilities from her peers, Arianh starts basking by the sea, where the others seldom venture for superstitious reasons. This only makes things worse, of course.

"She teases the sea serpent!" they say after watching Arianh throw a shell into the waves.

"I fear for my children!" they wail with the selfish righteousness of motherhood at every opportunity.

They all hate her: the women, the men, her husband, even her daughter. Eventually it becomes too much for Arianh to bear, for the truth is, she hates herself too. She hates what she's done, how stupid she was. But worst of all, she hates her role in Alek's transformation into the Suzerain.

VIII

In fairness, her role is a small one in the grand scheme of things, but she doesn't know it yet.

Alek had been away patrolling the Gharb's border for days, as was his usual whenever they fought, but he promised to be back for his daughter's birthday. He always keeps his promises to Ileana, so when the day arrives and he hasn't returned, Arianh knows something must have happened.

He did not come to me, Yewlow assures her.

Days pass and the people prepare for the worst. Except death is seldom that.

On one particularly hot morning, a boy finds Alek dragging himself across the rocks on the brink of dehydration with horrible wounds gouged in his calves and thighs. Once able to speak, he tells them how his party was ambushed by the Narrum and held captive for days to feed their hunger. He tells them how they started with the ones with more meat on their bones and hadn't bothered to ration – at first. Those men died quickly; the others, the lean ones like him, less so.

This is the first time someone survived the Narrum, and no one knows how to react. The people are shocked, horrified, but also utterly disgusted, and so the task of cleaning his wounds falls to Arianh. Not only because she's his wife, but because no one else dares to. More than once Arianh thinks she will faint, but she doesn't. His account of the events keeps her alert, and it will keep her awake for many nights afterwards.

Alek claims to have been conscious through the whole ordeal, and he describes to her in great detail how the Narrum butchered their flesh bit by bit, starting with the richer and less fatal areas, working their way to the bone, eating their flesh before their eyes while they still breathed. How they, upon believing one of his men to be dead, tossed what was left of him into the fire and then laughed at his screams while he burned. She remembers the Dharkan burning in Relicum and has to swallow the bile rising in her mouth. In that moment, she feels compassion for the man. She has no comforting words to give him though. She doubts there's even any able to comfort something like this, so she just cradles him in her arms.

"How did you escape?" she asks softy, soothing his hair.

He's silent for a long moment, shaking with pain and rage, then says, "There is no escape, love."

She stares at him then and recognises the change in his eyes for what it is. The man who returned is no longer her husband, Alek. This is the man she remembers – the Suzerain.

That night, while he sleeps, feverish and delirious from his wounds, she presses the dagger Freya gave her to his neck, convinced this is the reason she's travelled here – to kill him. To stop Alek Dveer from ever becoming the Suzerain. She wants to do it. By rights, she should be able to do it; spare Aegea his rule and spare him from his memories. It would be a kindness, she tells herself. No one should live through what he endured, and no one should endure what he would become. Not even the Narrum.

She is so sure of this, so committed, and yet she can't do it. The dagger trembles in her hand, resting against his throat – as close as it will go.

Yewlow, help me!

'I'm sorry. I cannot.'

Arianh curses the gods who made her kind unable to take a life even as a mercy and throws the dagger across the room.

Next morning, Alek wakes up with a new purpose: to protect his people at all costs. The Anann social guidelines become strict rules in the name of survival: Every able man has to patrol the Gharb. And every woman has to provide more men for the task. Those who are meek and obedient are well taken care of. Those who object are not worth their resources and, therefore, are exiled. It's as simple as that in his mind. His hair turns black at the temples over the next few days. The once fair and jovial leader becomes a tyrant. In the Gharb, caution turns to fear. And hope is lost entirely.

Alek's body heals remarkably quickly, but his mutilated calves never fully regenerate and prevent him from being able to accompany the scouts, and so he takes it upon himself to go house to house every day instead, making sure everyone is taken care of and are following his orders, then he walks along the beach, staring across the ocean as if he can see what lies beyond it. Sometimes he disappears for long periods of time. Arianh has no idea where to, only that each time, he returns angrier than before.

One day, he brings back company.

IX

Alek smiles at her as he enters their shelter. Since "the incident," Arianh has only seen him smile at Ileana, and even that is a rare sight. Taken by surprise, she smiles back. He wraps one arm around her shoulders – another surprise – and gestures to the entrance.

"Ann. I'd like you to meet someone." He points at a lithe man stepping shyly into the room. "This is Agnar."

"Agnar…" The blood rushes from her face; the smile dies on her lips. She feels dazed and has to sit down on her ankles to steady herself, picking up Ileana's scattered toys as an excuse to cover her reaction. "Apologies for the mess. Please, come in. I… I don't believe I've seen you here before," she says, searching for some sign of recognition on his part. There is none. For a brief moment Arianh hoped Agnar had followed her, but this man is much younger than the Agnar she knows, with long dark green hair and the bright eyes of a dreamer.

"No wonder. Agnar is a traitor to his people," Alek says, patting him hard on the back. "The smartest man in the Gharb and my best friend growing up."

"You never mentioned him before," Arianh points out.

"I mentioned a traitor, didn't I?" The tone defies contradiction.

Yes, he'd mentioned a traitor. Several, actually. Lately, anyone who disagrees with him is a traitor, so much so the word has almost lost its meaning.

"Agnar can't stand the place or anyone in it, am I right?" Agnar's body language expresses mortification rather than disagreement. "He's been gone since before you arrived. He just went for a walk by the coast one day and never returned. We'd given up on him! Everyone thought he died in pursuit of his endless quest for… for what, knowledge?" Alek leans closer to Agnar's ear. "A way out?" He laughs mockingly. "Turns out he's just been hiding in a hole all this time."

Arianh blinks at him.

"I... er... I found a network of caves far down the coast, running inland where the lava fields and the mountains meet. They are filled with texts and artefacts. Quite fascinating, really," Agnar offers as an explanation.

"Fascinating?" Alek laughs again.

Arianh shivers. She's heard that cruel laugh enough times to know how dangerous it is to be the cause of it.

"Agnar always liked to shelter in dark places. Even as a child, he rarely left his lair. Just like a Dharkan, huh?"

"Well… I wouldn't say –"

The laughter stops. "Did it ever occur to you to share the fascination with your best friend?" There is no more mirth in Alek's tone.

"Have you been living alone out there all this time?" Arianh asks, trying to spare him the answer.

"Yes," he murmurs.

"Why return now?"

Agnar looks sheepishly at Alek. "Nostalgia."

"And to share what he's learnt, of course. Agnar would never hide underground in the dark, keeping all the secrets to himself forever. That would be self-ish." Alek hits him on the shoulder again, harder this time. He stumbles forwards a step. His eyes meet hers. There's concern in his expression, embarrassment and something like regret, but definitely no recognition.

"I ran out of things to learn, so… I figured it was time to teach them to others," he says unconvincingly.

"Excellent! For I have a pupil for you." Alek points at Ileana, who sits on the floor, looking up at them open-mouthed.

"She's… young," Agnar says cautiously.

"Nonsense. She just turned five. I know what you're thinking, she's a girl, but she's the smartest girl in the Gharb. She takes after her father. A good thing, since my wife refuses to give me sons," Alek says pointedly.

"I'd rather share my knowledge with everyone," Agnar insists almost apologetically.

"I'm afraid that is not possible. *Everyone* is busy, you see. Besides, too much learning interferes with duty, just like thought interferes with labour. We can't have that. The Narrum are growing bolder and hun-grier. Ileana will be the one responsible for our people while I'm gone. She will learn from us, and then she'll chose someone to learn from her."

"Husband," Arianh says, biting back her anger. "An educated people is preferable to –"

Alek cuts her off. "Agnar will supervise Ileana's education from now on. It is decided."

She knows that tone well. There is nothing to be done but accept his decision. Alek was never a man easy to contradict, and after the incident, it's sensible to not even try.

"Well, then." Arianh forces a smile. "It is a pleasure to meet you, Agnar. I warn you, though, Ileana is a tough one to teach. She only pays attention to her hair."

Agnar smiles at her. She smiles at him.

Yewlow tuts.

X

For many days afterwards, Agnar, who apparently has always been of a frail disposition, spends most of his time indoors with Ileana and consequently with Arianh who, deprived of privacy and autonomy in the settlement, also prefers to stay indoors. They don't talk much at first. They have no need to. Silence is comfortable between them, and Agnar's company makes her happier than words can say.

One evening, the three are gathered in the same room. Arianh sips water from a cup while Ileana scratches something unidentifiable on a slab of schist. Arianh's eyes constantly drift from the girl to Agnar as he runs his fingertips across a scroll, brows furrowed with concentration.

"What is that?" Arianh finally asks, pointing at it. She's never seen such a script.

The question startles him. "I found it in the caves," he replies almost defensively.

"Can you read it?"

He scratches his head. "I… er… Honestly, I'm not

sure. The words are intelligible, their meaning, however…"

"What else did you find in those caves?" she asks.

His eyes drift from the page towards hers. "Bones… many, many bones…" he says absently, then shakes himself. "Alek tells me you came through the Chronodéndron."

The abrupt change of subject jars Arianh. Especially since the mere mention of travelling is now taboo under Alek's new rules. Then again, so is reading.

She clears her throat. "A long time ago," she says, as if that makes it irrelevant.

"Was the world different then?" he asks cautiously.

She sips her slightly briny water, regretting the fact she has no herbs to add flavour to it, and says, "Greener," in the same cautious tone.

"Ah, must have been beautiful. Have you ever tried to return?"

She shakes her head, then thinks better of it. "Many times," she admits.

"Why didn't you?"

"I can't. To most, chrono-travel is a one-way trip, it seems."

His enthusiasm dwindles. "Ah… yes. It's what the others said too."

"The others?"

"The ones who came before you. I talked to a few before they, er… gave up talking."

"I see…"

"You never did, though."

"I thought about it," she says truthfully.

He gives her a sad smile. "Everyone here thinks about it at least once a day, even without travelling."

They chuckle awkwardly.

It occurs to Arianh then that no one else has come through Yewlow since she arrived. Or if they did, Yewlow didn't mention it to her. Does this mean Chronos is truly gone, or that the Narrum got to them before they reached the Gharb? Neither option is worth considering.

"Can I ask... What did you pray for?" he asks.

For a moment, she just stares at him with tears in her eyes, remembering the time she asked him that very same question. "The wrong things," she eventually says.

He bobs his head slowly. "The others said the same, and yet they are gone and you're still here."

"I have something to hold on to," she says, looking at Ileana. The truth is, if not for Ambrosia and her link to Yewlow, she'd have killed herself long ago. Her life is a joyless succession of ugly days and even uglier tasks carried on through habit and necessity. Up until Agnar came along, she was numb, with no desires or expectations, only grief and regrets. Now, his presence has wakened something inside her. Something never quite forgotten.

Arianh stares back at him and sighs. "I wish I could just let go..." For some reason, she can't bring herself to lie to the man. Yet she can't tell him the truth either, so their conversations are usually a string of unfinished sentences.

Goddess, he must think I'm so dull.

He takes her hand and pats it gently, the way Odin used to do. Could it have been him behind the gesture all along?

"You are strong. The strong ones always suffer the most. But they are also the ones who survive."

Arianh snorts, remembering the time Occa told her she was as soft as pine wood. Had Occa taken her kingdom for herself in her absence? she wonders. Had she been strong enough to break it apart? Another thought not worth dwelling on.

"Agnar. I want to ask you something," she says before she can stop herself.

He gazes deeply into her eyes, expectantly. "Yes?"

"Who did you find in the caves?"

He blanches, lets go of her hand and stands up, scratching his head again. "No one alive," he says, avoiding her gaze.

Arianh nods once. *It seems neither lying nor telling the truth is an option for him, either.*

"Your time is up, young girl," she says to Ileana. "Show me what you did."

Ileana loves to draw but has no talent for it. Regardless, Arianh beams and says, "Oh, it's beautiful! Don't you think it's beautiful, Agnar?"

"You are." He flushes. "I mean, it is, of course it is. You both are. Apologies, I didn't mean to…"

"It's all right," she says. "A compliment never offended anyone."

"It might."

"Only if you're being honest." She grimaces at the ugly drawing behind Ileana's line of sight.

They laugh.

"Come, Ileana, time to sleep." She picks the girl up with some difficulty. She's growing too tall to be carried around for much longer.

"Perhaps I should go too," Agnar says half-heartedly.

"Please, stay. It's early and… Alek is on patrol. He won't be back until dawn." She doesn't wait for his reply, afraid of the disappointment it might cause.

When she returns, she finds him still leaning on the pillow, reading from a book. Her eyes widen. It's unmistakably one of Seshat's, and the word *Nephilim* written on the cover escapes her lips before she can stop herself.

He blinks. "You can read?"

There's no point denying it. "Yes."

"Are women allowed to learn such a skill when you come from?"

"Well… yes."

"Does Alek –"

"No." She sits by his side. "You found this in the caves? Are there more?"

Agnar closes the book, then shuffles uncomfortably, as if trying to put some space between them. The innocent awkwardness of moments before replaced by wariness and a whole different kind of curiousness. "Is written knowledge accessible to everyone when you came from?"

"Er… no. I was privileged," she admits. Of course, she can't tell him exactly how privileged. "My uncle taught me." It's easier to think of the Wyrd as Odin now, not Uncle, but under the circumstances, naming gods is definitely not an option.

"Was he an important man?"

Goddess, this is maddening. It's bad enough to be staring at the man. She'd rather not talk about the one who would take over his body in a few years.

She takes a deep breath to collect herself. "He was a wise man," she says truthfully for a change. "He reminds me of you. Knowledge was his passion, and he was kind enough to share some of it with me." She sighs. "Agnar, I know my husband prohibits it, but I want you to teach Ileana to read. You're teaching her everything else. It would be faster and more efficient if she learnt to read properly instead of drawing pictographs. I would do it, but… if Alek finds out I –" She stops herself, covering her mouth. "You won't tell him, will you?"

His eyes widen in something like indignation. "Never. You have my word. But I can't teach her either, Ann. I'm sorry. The rules are clear: no writing. It's not the sort of thing that can be kept secret. Ileana wouldn't be able to keep it a secret, I mean. Alek would find out one way or another. Maybe when she's older…" His tone suggests scepticism. He knows well how much the girl worships her father.

Arianh presses her lips together and doesn't insist on the matter.

"I will teach her all I know through stories. It will suffice," he says.

"Stories are easy to forget."

"Not how I tell them." He winks. "And I'll tell them as often as I must. She'll learn."

"You don't understand," Arianh says.

"Explain it to me."

"She *will* forget."

Understanding dawns in his eyes. Or at least she hopes it does. Either that or he's thinking she'd probably be better off shattered at the bottom of a cliff.

He sits back, looking very serious. "Ann, why do you think Alek forbids people to learn how to read and write properly?"

"Because he's rotten. He wants to keep all knowledge to himself, so he can control others," she replies, letting all her pent-up hatred for the man surge through the words. She can't help herself.

Agnar's expression is one of deep sadness. "Yes…" He tilts his head. "And no. You see, the written word is dangerous. Out of context, even facts can be treacherous. Imagine if everyone knew how to write. Then anyone could write about whatever they want, fill entire manuscripts with nonsense and lies. Then imagine, many years later, others might find and read that nonsense and, without knowing any better, take those lies as truth. They might even arrange their whole lives, their belief systems, society and culture around them." He shakes his head. "The consequences could be catastrophic."

"What about the truth? Actual truth is worth recording, so it's not forgotten. So we don't have to go through the same trials, repeat the same mistakes as our ancestors," Arianh insists.

"Truth is in the mind. We have eyes to see, brains to think. We have all we need to know the truth. And we have memory to remember it. But once it's written, truth is indistinguishable from lies."

She chuckles the way Seshat often did. "I knew someone who would have emphatically disagreed with you."

"How so?"

"Memories can be lost. Or worse, changed. They're even less reliable than words on a scroll. The only way to keep the truth intact is to write it down in stone."

He considers this. "Perhaps. But how can we trust the person writing it?"

Arianh didn't think that one through. He has a point. How could she trust the average mortal to keep an objective record of anything? Or worse, a god? She realises he knows nothing about the inscrutable chronicler. *Oh, frost…* She shakes her head and points at the book in his lap. "Do you believe what's written in there?"

He hesitates, weighing the book in his hands. "I believe it's always easier to learn fake truths than to forget the real ones. Knowledge is flawed. But wisdom goes beyond memory, beyond record. It's linked to our souls."

"We don't have souls," Arianh says dryly.

"Who told you that?"

The goddess of the soul, she wants to say. "Just trust me on that one."

"Well, we must have something. Gaea's spirit, if nothing else. Otherwise, how do you explain this?"

He holds her hand again, caressing her fingertips. "Memory works through touch and scent and taste, not just vision and hearing. There's more information about who we are and how we feel shared in moments through our fingertips than put into words in an entire book. This is not memory. It's not in our minds. It's within us. The next time we touch, I'll remember us as we are now. In this moment."

"Promise?" she whispers. *Did he?* she wonders. Then she remembers she was wearing a different face back then. *No, of course not, you fool.*

He answers her question with a kiss.

XI

Arianh tells herself afterwards that what happened was inevitable and meant little, just a mere taste of what could have been between Agnar and her back at the forest. She tells herself that she only did it because she was lonely and needed the comfort. That is all true enough. As is the fact that she desperately needs Agnar to remember her. If her past would be his future, she wants him to want her enough to stop her from travelling. She no longer believes she will return, so the best she can do is make sure she never leaves in the first place.

Alek finds out what happened, of course. He all but set them up, leaving the two alone night after night so he could use their feelings as leverage while appearing righteous in his punishments. The very next day, he sends Agnar away from the settlement and keeps him engaged in "research," while personally taking over Ileana's education. He doesn't teach her how to write, though, even after he makes Agnar teach him both the Aesir and the Olympian scripts.

Arianh's loneliness increases tenfold. At first she's certain Alek will exile her, but he never does. He's either too proud or too mean to give her her freedom. She thinks the latter is more likely. It's like he feeds on her misery. She and Agnar still manage to steal a few moments of clandestine happiness now and again, but mostly she spends her days alone by the shore; watching the tumultuous grey ocean soothes her own turbulent mind.

Meanwhile, Alek's love for Ileana turns to obsession. There's nothing he wouldn't do or give to the girl because, as he often puts it, she's their future. He even allows her to attend the council meetings. The exceptional treatment makes Ileana grow entitled and vain. She's devoted to her role and precocious, but not particularly clever. She believes her privileges result from her being special, and she revels in the people's attention, especially the boys. Arianh warns her about playing with men's lust. Not because she thinks Ileana is in any danger, mind, not at that age, and no man would ever dare to lay a finger on her for fear of her father. Nevertheless, her reckless behaviour grates on Arianh, and any attempts to correct her daughter's demeanour only makes the girl disobey her more. Eventually, she gives up.

One day she's returning from bathing in the shallows when she crosses the path of a boy. Normally children would pretend not to see her – at their parents' command – but this one is an orphan, and he actually stops to let her through the narrow path ahead of him. Not out of respect or fear, but courtesy. He's skinny, with bleached olive hair and skin already showing the first signs of sun damage, but there's something in his demeanour that sets him apart from the other children besides the tragic death of his parents, or more precisely, makes the other boys set him apart from them. He doesn't seem too bothered by it though, for he seems to prefer playing with the girls, anyway.

"Good dawn, Lady Ann. May the sun be gentle on your skin," the boy says with a bright smile.

She freezes, her heart pounding in her chest. She's seen him before. There aren't that many children in the Gharb, after all. He's one of Ileana's friends, but she never allowed herself to actually *see* the boy. She sure does now.

Stammering, she says, "Good day, Jud – er, I'm sorry, I've forgotten your name," she lies, unable to think of anything else to say or take her eyes off the boy.

Freezing goddess! She has not thought about Judoc in years, to the point she hasn't even considered the possibility of meeting him again. Certainly not like this.

"My name is Iosh, Lady Ann." He already possesses the glint in his eyes that will later make so many girls swoon in his presence.

"Right," she chokes. "It's a lovely name," she says truthfully, wondering why he changed it. *Probably for similar reasons I did.*

He grins again and gives her a coy glance as he walks away.

"Wait," she calls after him, working hard to collect herself.

He walks back to her, intrigued. "Yes, Lady Ann?"

She kneels so their eyes are at the same level. He keeps smiling that boyish grin of his, only at this age it's still innocent and honest, free of mischief or intent. It breaks her heart.

She wants to say things like: "You're a kind boy, Iosh. Stay good and be strong. Don't let them change you. I loved you so much!" But how can she? The words die in her throat, and she pulls herself together.

"Listen to me very carefully," she says.

The boy's smile vanishes at the harsh tone, and he gives her his full attention.

"Stay the frost away from my daughter." She grabs his arms and shakes him hard enough to make an impression. "Do you understand me?"

The boy staggers, bewildered and afraid. "I-I didn't hurt her. We just kissed, I swear. She likes me!"

Oh goddess, it's already too late!

She slaps him. "Do not kiss her again! Ever. My husband will kill you if he finds out, but before he does, I'll" – she shows him the ebony dagger she carries strapped to her thigh at all times – "I'll chop your manhood off. Understand?"

The boy begins to cry, pries himself free from her grip and runs inland.

She closes her eyes, bracing herself on the ground. *Frost! What have I done?* Arianh knows she can no longer stay in the settlement after this. Word of her outburst will spread, validating her reputation as a crazy woman and vindicating the many mothers who think her unsuitable to be around their children. She can't live surrounded by so many ghosts, so many enemies. Ileana and Iosh will soon be past the age when memory can be dismissed as childhood fantasy. She has to leave, before retaliations, before Alek finds out and gets even more suspicious of her origin. Then she remembers this day marks Ileana's eighth birthday. Isn't that just the final failure of Arianh as a mother: to abandon her only child on her birthday? But that's exactly what she does without even a goodbye, convincing herself it's the best option for both of them.

She leaves her the obsidian dagger, as Freya instructed, and a note to Alek, saying she's going to the shadow. It ends with "Do not follow." She leaves nothing for Agnar but his memories.

Only some time afterwards does it occur to her that maybe it would have been better if everyone thought she'd drowned. Her best ideas always happen in hindsight. And yet the relief she feels as she runs along the shore, each step taking her further away from the Gharb and those living in it, overcomes any guilt she might feel for leaving.

It's what I should have done a long time ago, she tells herself. Then she realises she never really thought of Ileana as her daughter. How could she? In her mind, as in so many other ways, she's always been Alek's.

She stops running.

It's my fault. The Suzerain's treatment of women, his relationship with Ileana, her personality. Maybe even Judoc's personality. It's all my fault.

'Talk about self-importance, queen,' Yewlow says reproachfully.

If I hadn't come here, Ileana wouldn't exist. She wouldn't have travelled. None of this would have happened!

'And yet you're here because it did happen.'

Arianh isn't listening. *It is my fault. My ambition did this. Oh, goddess!*

'Might as well blame your mother for raising you to be a queen. The gods for bringing the Aossi to Aegea in the first place. And me, of course me, for bringing you here.'

I do blame you!

'How's that working out for you?'

"Aargh!" she screams to the ocean.

Something screams back.

XII

Three days later, Alek prays at the Chronodéndron for the first time.

Yewlow relays his prayers to Arianh. Some of them, at least. Arianh suspects there's a lot the tree still doesn't tell her, but what she does keeps her mind entertained while she walks. After four more days walking along the shore and another two across the barren land, Arianh finally arrives at Agnar's caves. Despite her wishes and her experience on the beach, Yewlow is adamant it's not Arianh's time to return yet, so the caves are as far as she goes. She hopes to find one of the gods here, or even Aedan – not that she knows what she will say to him, or anyone, for that matter. It just… would be nice to see a familiar face. But there is none. She finds nothing but books she can't read, broken pieces of things she can't put together and bones – so many bones… it's as if the whole of Aegea went there to die.

How appropriate…

There's still water deep within the rock and plenty of shade. Whatever killed these people was not thirst or the elements, and looking at their shattered remains, she's inclined to think they killed each other. The idea doesn't perturb her half as much as it would have years before, not even half as much as it should. She just shrugs it off and takes residence in one of the least cluttered spaces.

During the next few days, Arianh collects every manuscript she can find, and over the next few years, she learns to read them all. Even the ones in Seshat's most convoluted handwriting. What she learns shocks her.

I have to go back, she insists to Yewlow almost daily. *Most Narrum must have died of starvation by now, so the risk of travel over the ridge is minimal.*

'*Not yet,*' is always the reply.

I need to warn them!

'*You will.*'

When?

'*Soon.*'

AARGH! I've done everything you asked!

'*Yes, and I need you to do one more thing.*'

"What?!" Arianh's exasperated question echoes through the cavern.

'*I need you to wait.*'

∞

More years pass – six in total, according to the scratches she makes on the rock every dawn – when she spots Agnar coming up the hill. Arianh is about to run out to meet him when she sees he's not alone. Ileana is with him, grown into a younger version of the woman Arianh met in Relicum. She searches for a resemblance, something of herself in the girl, but finds only Alek's features.

Arianh watches from afar as Agnar, to the best of his ability, educates his "niece" about the origins of her people. Ileana seems interested, eager to learn, and most importantly, happy with Agnar. Arianh no longer punishes herself for leaving, nor does she give much thought to how her absence affected the girl. To the best of her knowledge, she had a privileged life – or as privileged as life could be in the Gharb – right up to the point when Psyche would take her. Then again, that was hardly Arianh's fault. Seeing Ileana now brings a certain… closure, since comfort has long since become an alien concept for her.

She hasn't seen or talked to another person in years and is considering going to them – Yewlow's wishes be damned – when a hand lands on her shoulder.

"Aaah!"

Arianh jumps and turns around. The man standing behind her is stern and sinewy, like an old warrior. He has long grey hair streaked with blond, same as his beard, and wears a grey cloak, a walking staff and a patch over his right eye.

"Hello, dear."

"Uncle?!"

"Call me Odin."

"I thought you were in the Underworld."

"Maybe I am." His eye bores into her. "I see Freya got to you first."

"She did indeed. I'm not your niece anymore. Do you like what she's done?"

"My opinion is irrelevant."

"Why did she do it?"

"Because she could." He leans on his staff as if tired.

"My wife has her plans and ways. They rarely coincide with mine. We've been married for aeons and I still don't understand her. She wants to change things. So do I. But the things she wants to change are not the same as the ones I do."

The wicked twinkle in his eye makes the hairs on Arianh's nape stand on end both with apprehension and revulsion.

"You should have interfered sooner, then," she tells him.

"And you should have never been born."

"How dare you!"

"It's the truth."

Goddess, she wants to hit him. If the cruel creature standing in front of her is the real Odin, Agnar's influence on the Wyrd definitely went way beyond a few mannerisms.

He cares nothing for her outrage. "What's done is done. What happened will happen. I only came to give you something."

"I don't want anything from you," she spits.

In a blink of an eye, he snatches her hand and forces it open with a strength more telepathic than physical, then places a pouch in it. "Take this to your father."

She looks at the pouch, opens it, and would have dropped it had he not forced her hand closed around it with his.

"It's important."

"You're mad. You gods are all mad! Freezing goddess, what is the meaning of this? Are you mocking me? Is my suffering amusing to you? Hasn't it been enough already? And I don't even know who my father is!"

"You will."

"I hope you freeze in the shadow!"

"I already have." He turns to leave, then halts, keeping his back towards her. "For all it's worth, I do wish things had been different, Arianh. But a god's wishes are as good as a mortal's in this Universe." He fades away as he walks.

Down the hill, Agnar and Ileana are already gone. They do not return.

∞

After that fated encounter, Arianh has nothing left to do but wait. She waits while Yewlow carries Alek and Ileana across time; she's still waiting after the tree brings them back, changed. She keeps waiting long after Agnar and Iosh go through. She feels their spirits touching hers as Yewlow carries them across, and then their absence nearly destroys her. After that, she feels nothing for many years except bitter regret for her choices and her ambitions of longevity.

One dawn, as Arianh tries to bask without burning herself raw, Yewlow bursts into her mind. *'It's time!'*

Arianh sends a mental *hmm?* to the tree.

'Time to go. Now!'

Arianh doesn't move. It's been years – almost decades! – with barely a word from the Chronodéndron, left waiting alone on the verge of insanity, and suddenly Yewlow is in a hurry? Well, whatever it is, it can surely wait until sunset.

A shadow appears over her. "Get up, girl!"

"Freezing goddess!" Arianh grabs a rock and rolls away from Freya, ready for anything.

"Oh, my! Have you turned feral already?" the Dharkan crone cackles. "It's only been a few years."

"Thirty-four."

Freya shrugs. "Like I said: only a few. You look good for a middle-aged dryad."

Arianh grits her teeth; her jaw aches with the strain of avoiding speaking her mind. "How the –" *Breathe.* "Where the frost have you been all this time?"

"Waiting. Same as you."

The goddess looks older for sure. Her skin is no longer leathery but thin and sallow as if made of wax. She wears her long, feathered cloak with a hood capable of blocking even the harsh Aegean sun. Still, only a god would be so bold (or foolish) to walk under it wearing a Dharkan.

Huginn and Muninn land on her shoulder.

Arianh never thought she'd feel such joy again. "They're alive!"

"As opposed to what?"

Arianh's eyes rest on Freya's feather cloak again.

"This? You thought I –?" She cackles. "They are too useful for that. Aren't you, little rascals?"

The ravens caw in unison, though it's hard to tell if in indignation or agreement.

Arianh drops the rock. She's too tired to fight, too relieved to be angry, but too hurt to forgive, either. "Has it ever occurred to you that maybe we could have waited together?"

Freya's white eyebrows rise up her forehead. "Why would we do that to ourselves?"

"I don't know. Company?" Arianh suggests bitterly.

The Dharkan crone laughs, and suddenly her stance, eye colour, and even her voice, change. "I know the living can't handle solitude, but would you really have preferred to spend two decades inside a cave with a Wraith for company, *dryad*?"

Arianh recoils, realisation dawning on her. "You're not Freya."

The Dharkan closes her eyes and takes a deep breath. "I am myself. Iva just likes to remind me I'm not *in* myself. You think solitude is bad, imagine an eternity spent with someone who hates you."

She'd rather not. "Why don't you leave her?"

"It's complicated." Freya's sigh defines weariness, so Arianh doesn't press the subject. Anything involving gods and Wraiths has to be complicated, and she has enough complications of her own.

"Come, I'll tell you everything you need to know on the way," the goddess says.

"Where are we going?"

'*To me,*' Yewlow replies.

XIII

They arrive at the Chronodéndron shortly after Ileana and Ideth, and Arianh has to cover her mouth to muffle the emotional cross between a gasp and a cry when she sees them. Yewlow warns her not to interfere, under any circumstances, so all she can do is watch in wide-eyed confusion as Ideth disappears, and in terror when Ileana begins opening her veins with the dagger she gave her.

Arianh glares at Freya, prepared to put an end to her daughter's madness. The goddess, who without the cover of her hood looks more Dharkan than ever, renders her immobile with her will again. Whatever the disagreement between her and her host, it's obviously convenient enough to allow her to use at least some of her powers. The cruel goddess doesn't even leave Arianh enough agency to close her eyes or look away from the scene – a scene she would never understand had she not simultaneously experienced it through her link with Yewlow.

The moment Ileana travels, something in the surrounding scenery seems to ripple, and suddenly, to Arianh's eyes, it's like there're more stars in the sky.

Freya leaves their hiding space and drags Arianh towards the Chronodéndron to stand amidst the gods.

"Do you think she bought it?" Prometheus asks.

"I was thorough," the goddess holding the torch replies, then her face breaks into three. Arianh blinks as everything about her changes.

"Are you sure?" he insists.

"Yes," she replies with impatience. "The dagger still had enough of Mnemosyne's talent to power the spell."

"Still, Psyche's mind –"

"She bought it! Look up." The gods look at the sky, then glare at each other for a moment.

"So it is done," Freya says, deflating.

"What is done?" Arianh asks, still fixated on the strange deities. Yewlow's translation of events only goes so far.

"Ileana has a soul now. *The* soul," Freya explains.

"Are you kidding me? Is this what it was all about? She had it before!" Arianh shouts. "Nothing's changed. You just sent her and Psyche on the same journey as before!"

"Change takes time," the three-faced goddess snorts pointedly. "And time's against it."

"Have faith, Hecate," Prometheus says. "The right path will prevail. I still know a few tricks." He doesn't sound too certain, though, and she doesn't look too convinced.

"Humph," Freya says. "None of this would have happened without you and your friend's *tricks*."

"But it did! Do you want to keep arguing about it for eternity?"

"What else is left to do?" Freya grumbles.

"You're free to go now, dryad. Your prayers have been answered. Your part in this is complete," Prometheus says, dismissing the old goddess.

Arianh blinks. First he ignores her, now he addresses her as if they were old acquaintances. "Go where?" she asks him through clenched teeth.

"Wherever you wish. Yewlow will know where to take you."

Where would she go? She can't go back to her old life wearing this face. But she certainly doesn't want to stay here, either. She has no home, no identity, no friends. No sanity left. She's a used-up, dried husk of a creature linked to a tree who knows too much and does too little.

"I have nowhere to go. My life is ruined," she says, realising that after so long, if it's not the truth, it sure feels like it.

"Mortal, you know nothing of ruin," Hecate says matter-of-factly. "Use what you've learned wisely and you will prevail." She turns to Freya. "Are you ready?"

Freya nods and whispers something to the ravens. They fly to Arianh's shoulder. "Take good care of them, girl. Next time we meet each other, I will not remember you. And I will not be kind."

You never were! Arianh thinks angrily.

"Where are you goin –" Before Arianh can finish the question, Freya and Hecate vanish into thin air. She'd seen Hades and Hel translocate many times, but this looks different. Like when Odin disappeared back at the caves, they leave something of an after-image behind them, slowly fading away like the memory of a dream upon wakening.

Only Prometheus remains, staring at her as if contemplating what to say or waiting for her to say something to him. Arianh knows who he is, thanks to Yewlow. And she also knows what he has done. That, she learned along with her father's identity from the records at the cave, and she's not impressed. She feels nothing but contempt for the god who created the Narrum.

"Prometheus." She utters the name with loathing. "What do you have to say for yourself?" There's no need to elaborate. She's sure he can read her mind well enough.

"I've paid the price." His voice and demeanour remind her of Chiron: always so gentle, patient and polite – even as he tried to rip her jaw off.

"The entire Universe has," Arianh says truthfully. She feels no pity or nausea contemplating the gaping wound in his stomach. Well, at least she's finally got over *that* particular weakness.

He sighs. "Yes... But thanks to you and others like you, there is still hope to make amends."

"I wish you hadn't used me for the task."

"As do I." He sounds sincere. Then again, gods usually do. "Speaking of wishes…" He goes down on his knees, startling Arianh into silence. "You once wished for a god's respect. And now you have it." He holds her hand in both of his and bows his forehead to it. When he raises it again, he has moisture in his eyes. "You are a true queen, Arianh. Your kind deserved more from us than being annihilated by humans. I'm sorry I did not see it before."

"Er…" Arianh says, overwhelmed by the Titan's words.

"I will ask one more thing of you, my queen."

Ah, there it is – the price, she thinks to herself. Gods give nothing for free, not even compliments.

"When you find Loki, tell him… I'm sorry."

This is unexpected. "Sorry for what?"

The god hesitates a moment, then grimaces. "Better to let him choose."

And with that, he's gone, just like the others. Her hand falls limp beside her, his touch only a memory.

'Now it's your turn,' Yewlow says. *'All your wishes have been fulfilled. You are free to make new ones. I suggest you be more sensible this time. Also, be aware of how you articulate them. Better not to give me much room for creativity.'*

"You are in my head! You know what I wish better than I do."

'True. But I've also been planted here for longer than most gods have been alive. I'm bored. Twisting wishes keeps me lush.'

"You're evil."

'I'm a tree. I can't neither be good nor evil. Now, shall I take you back to when you left? Agnar is still waiting for you, by the way.'

He is?! Arianh stills herself and turns to face the Chronodéndron's twisted trunk. "Then you lied to me!" she accuses the tree out loud.

'No, I didn't. I can't lie. I just didn't tell you everything, and in my defence, you never asked.'

"That's your excuse? I never asked. I've asked you thousands of questions!"

'Just not the right ones.'

Arianh's frustration is too strong for this conversation. "I set this all in motion. If I hadn't come here,

Ileana wouldn't have been born. Alek would never have reason to pray to you! You knew how much I suffered. How often I wondered, and you never even told me he was waiting for me!"

'Would that have helped? You were so anxious, so distraught. Had you known he was waiting and hoped to return, wouldn't it have made the wait worse? Besides, you started nothing. All this already happened, you just experienced it from a different perspective.'

"You used me."

'I'm only a tree.'

"Then the gods used me."

'It had to be done.'

"Stop saying that! Nothing of what I did *had* to be done. This was never about me, my people, or even the Narrum. It was always about the gods and their quests for power over each other."

'You are partly right. This is not about one person, race or world. This involves the whole universe. You and everyone on this rock don't matter. Thousands of dead gods and trillions of mortals in the Underworld don't matter. All that matters is that the cycle's been broken.'

Arianh wants to scream. *Broken into what?* she wants to say, instead she says, "How can it be broken if we keep taking the same actions, making the same mistakes?"

'Not the same. We make different ones each time, and this time we did it right.'

"How can you be sure?"

'I have faith.'

Now Arianh wants to laugh. "Faith? Is that the best you've got? Gods never rely on faith."

'*I'm not a god,*' Yewlow says. '*Now, remember to stay alive, for both our sakes.*'

Arianh's hand lifts by its own accord to touch Yewlow's bark. She closes her eyes, takes a deep breath and tries to visualise Agnar as she last saw him before she travelled all those years ago. When she opens them again, she sees him smiling at her.

"Welcome back, Ann."

And for the first time in years, she smiles.

Acknowledgements

I'd like to thank my husband, Dave, for his unyielding support and for not sparing any ink on his red pen while reading this first draft.

A huge thank you to all the bloggers and reviewers who helped bring Timelessness to the spotlight, especially Fantasy Book Nerd and Vesna S.

To my editor, Lisa Gilliam, for once again fixing my errors and putting all those commas, quotation marks and tenses in order.

To Sarah Kempton for her outstanding narration of the first three books. I look forward to listening to this one.

To all the friends, readers and strangers who reached out with encouraging words of appreciation and support. I keep writing because of you guys!

To everyone who took the time to write a review and share their thoughts about this series with the world, especially Ana C. Reis for her friendship and all the marketing tips, Ian Bannon for his book recommendations and putting up with my mini rants, Alan Scott for his enthusiasm for the audiobooks, Dan, who probably didn't know what he was getting into when he requested that code, and Mike for all the times he liked, shared and recommended my books on Twitter.

And to Locke for abdicating his favourite spot on the couch while I write.